Grandma's House Is Haunted

Stephen G. Bowling

Illustrated by Vitali Dudarenka

www.StephenGBowling.com

Dedicated to my father Ray Bowling, who always
helped make the world a little less scary.

Also by Stephen G. Bowling and Vitali Dudarenka
Simon's Tree House Adventures Series
Simon's Tree Party
Simon's Search for the Scary Dragon
Simon's Rocket to the Moon

and

Calvin the Christmas Tree

Publisher's Cataloging-in-Publication Data

Names: Bowling, Stephen G., 1960- author. | Dudarenka, Vitali, 1965- illustrator.
Title: Grandma's house is haunted / Stephen G. Bowling ; Vitali Dudarenka, illustrator.
Description: Stamford, CT : Valley of Mexico, 2022. | Summary: The children think Grandma's creaky
    old house is haunted and she doesn't know it. | Audience: Grades K-3.
Identifiers: LCCN 2022916364 (print) | ISBN 978-1-950957-24-8 (paperback) | ISBN 978-1-950957-25-5
    (hardcover) | ISBN 978-1-950957-26-2 (Kindle ebook) | ISBN 978-1-950957-27-9 (epub ebook)
Subjects: LCSH: Picture books for children. | CYAC: Bedtime--Fiction. | Halloween--Fiction. | Ghosts-
    -Fiction. | Grandmothers--Fiction. | Fear--Fiction. | BISAC: JUVENILE FICTION / Bedtime &
    Dreams. | JUVENILE FICTION / Holidays & Celebrations / Halloween. | JUVENILE FICTION /
    Ghost Stories. | JUVENILE FICTION / Readers / Beginner.
Classification: LCC PZ7.1.B69 Gr 2022 (print) | LCC PZ7.1.B69 Gr 2022 (ebook) | DDC [E]--dc23.

Copyright © 2023 Stephen G. Bowling

Valley of Mexico, Inc., Stamford, CT
info@valleyofmexico.com

www.StephenGBowling.com

A sleepover at Grandma's is always a treat.
She makes cookies and cakes
and fun things to eat.

She plays all our games and reads all our books.
She makes us both laugh
with funny face looks.

But when the eve comes
and darkness has followed,
our eyes open wide,
our courage is swallowed.

Her house comes alive
and makes creepy sounds,
as goblins come out
and are making their rounds.

It's scary at night,
things move by themselves.
Shadows reveal creatures
who live on the shelves.

Doors move without help
and speak in strange tones.
They move back and forth
as if they have bones.

There are specters about,
of that we are certain,
and a furry-faced dragon
who lives in the curtain.

A fiend in the shadows
wears a hat with a feather.
There are beasts in the basement
who are dancing together.

We see wolves wearing raincoats
and bats standing tall.
We hear running in the attic
where devils play ball.

Witches at windows
make strange noises outside.
Little creatures fly around them,
oddly shaped and big eyed.

Hobgoblins above
stretch the whole ceiling long,
and ghosts in the walls
moan together in song.

When we told her our scares, Grandma then smiled.
"There's nothing to fear,
just your imaginations run wild.

Dim lights can play tricks on young minds that it seems,
but long monsters on ceilings
are only the beams.

Peculiar sounds all around play tricks in your ear,
a settling old house
the odd noises you hear."

"There are no ghoulies or ghosties
or long-legged bats.
There are no phantoms with umbrellas
or monsters with hats.

There are no goblins or ghouls
that move things about,
no spirits who sing
and flow from the spout."

"There are no ogres with bumps
or dragons with hair,
a few knick-knacks and clocks,
that's all that is there.
Creatures in closets
are coats on their hooks,
and devils with pitchforks
only pencils and books."

"Things move from the wind,
some houses are leaky.
Rusty hinges need oil
to make them less squeaky.

Noises on windows,
simply taps from the trees.
Small creatures flying about,
merely leaves in the breeze."

"The pipes in the walls
make the groans and the growls.
The plumbing, you see,
makes loud noises and howls.

Those thumps that you hear
neither dancing nor games,
just a settling old house,
creaking sounds from the frames."

"Now time for bed,
    there's nothing to fear.
    Us and the cats,
        the only ones here.

It's just an old house,
    we can settle on that.
    Now lay down your heads,
        let's be done with our chat."

"Sleep well grandchildren,
you don't need the light.
Tomorrow's a new day
and all will be right."

We went to sleep
all snug in our beds.
We now understood
it was all in our heads.

Next time you're afraid
you should listen to me.
There are no ghoulies or ghosties
of that you will see.

See more at www.StephenGBowling.com

Also by Stephen G. Bowling and Vitali Dudarenka

Simon's Tree House Adventures Series

Simon's Tree Party

Simon's Search for the Scary Dragon

Simon's Rocket to the Moon

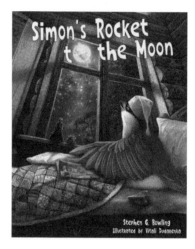

*Calvin
the
Christmas Tree*

Sign up for our email list and get news,

previews, free stuff and more.

www.StephenGBowling.com

Printed in the USA
CPSIA information can be obtained
at www.ICGtesting.com
BVHW010025210823
668717BV00014BA/121